The Best Halloween of All

Susan Wojciechowski
illustrated by Susan Meddaugh

CANDLEWICK PRESS

For my mother,
who still dresses up on Halloween
S. W.

For Niko, Jonathan, and Daniel
S. M.

Text copyright © 1998 by Susan Wojciechowski
Illustrations copyright © 1992 by Susan Meddaugh

First U.S. edition in this format 2012

The Library of Congress has cataloged the hardcover edition as follows:
Wojciechowski, Susan.
The best Halloween of all / Susan Wojciechowski ;
illustrated by Susan Meddaugh. — 2nd ed.
p.   cm.
Summary: A young boy recalls all the Halloween costume agonies he's been through,
until, at last, he gets to do things his own way!
ISBN 978-0-7636-0458-5 (hardcover)
[1. Halloween — Fiction. 2. Costume — Fiction.] I. Meddaugh, Susan, ill. II. Title.
PZ7.W8183Be   1998
[E] — dc21   97-18209
ISBN 978-0-7636-1241-2 (paperback)
ISBN 978-0-7636-6008-6 (reduced paperback)

12 13 14 15 16 17 SCP 10 9 8 7 6 5 4 3 2 1
Printed in Humen, Dongguan, China

This book was typeset in Providence-Sans.
The illustrations were done in watercolor, colored pencil, and ink.

Candlewick Press
99 Dover Street
Somerville, Massachusetts 02144

visit us at www.candlewick.com

Ben — 1 year

My family has a photo album with pictures of me and my big brother in every one of our Halloween costumes. For **my first Halloween** I was a clown. In the picture, I'm trying to yank the pointy clown hat off my head.

"I don't look very happy," I said one day when we were all looking at the pictures.

"Oh, it was a wonderful Halloween," my mom said.
"We showed you off to your grandma."

"Gran gave me a dollar and three candy apples,"
said my brother, Michael.

"What did I get?" I asked.
"You got a hug," said Mom.
"Did I have fun?"

"You cried most of the ride home," Michael
told me. "Then you fell asleep and drooled
all over your costume."

Michael- 4 years

Ben – 2 years

When I was **two years old,** Michael was
a magician and I was his rabbit for Halloween.
Mom sewed Michael an awesome black cape.
She made me a scratchy white rabbit suit.
At every house, my brother waved his
magic wand over a top hat my dad made.
I was supposed to jump up from behind it.
"You never did," said Michael.

"Maybe I didn't feel like jumping that day," I said.

When I was **three years old,** Mom decided my brother and I should be an angel and a devil for Halloween.

Since Michael is older, he got to choose which one he wanted to be.

Guess who had to dress up in a
gown and wear a coat hanger halo
and dumb cardboard wings?

Michael and Ben

Ben - 3 years

Michael –
6 years

Ben – 4 years

When I was **four years old,** Michael was
a mouse and I was a wedge of Swiss cheese for
Halloween. Dad made my costume out of wood.

"The problem was, your costume weighed so
much you couldn't walk up anyone's steps,"
said Michael, laughing.

"The problem was," I said, "Dad told
you to ask for candy for me, and at three
houses you forgot!"

When I was five years old, I was a robot for Halloween and Michael was the scientist who created me.

Ben – 5 years

Michael – 7 years

Dad made my costume out of a cardboard box that he painted silver. He brought switches and dials and control knobs from work and glued them all over the box.

"I worked on that costume every night for two weeks," said Dad, "but it was worth it."

At every house, my brother was supposed to push one of my buttons, and I was supposed to say **"Trick or treat"** in a robot voice.

"I remember that the box was so hot inside I had to take it off and carry it after two houses," I said.

"You ruined all the fun," said Michael.

When I was **six years old,** Mom decided
I would be a bunch of grapes for Halloween and
spent a week sewing the costume.

"That was the best Halloween costume
in the history of the world!" Mom said.
    Mom was wrong.
    It was **the worst costume** she ever
came up with.

At my classroom party, Claire, Sarah, and Katherine asked me what I was supposed to be. Calvin looked at me funny.

Max said, "You belong inside Fruit of the Loom underwear."
I couldn't sit down all afternoon because of the grapes sewed to my behind.

The photo album had
no more Halloween pictures
after that because **my seventh
Halloween** was still a month
away. As soon as we closed the
album, I started to worry about
what my parents might be
dreaming up.

Finally, I decided I had to do something. I walked into the family room one night and announced, "This year I want to make my own costume."

Mom said, "But, Ben, honey, we always help
with your costume."

"I know," I said, "but I think I can do it myself.
Is that okay?"

"Sure," Mom said, and gave me a hug.

This Halloween I was an intergalactic-space-starship robotron armed with a laser-pulverizer-beam rod.

I made the costume out of a grocery bag and some paper towel rolls.

It was the best Halloween of all.